See you when I see you

CONTENTS

See you when I see you

Rose Lagercrantz

Eva Eriksson

Peachtree

GECKO PRESS

....

PART I

Chapter 1

The summer break was over and it was time for
Dani to start her second year of school.

"I can't understand how you've grown so big!"
said her grandmother as they walked to school on
the first day.

Dani wasn't sure how it had happened, either.

But by the second day she was already used to it.

And by the time the class went to Skansen Zoo, as students Dani's age usually did, it was as if Dani had always been in her second year of school.

By then, Dani's father was home from the hospital, where he had been the whole summer after his traffic accident.

One of his legs would never be completely right, the doctor said.

But for Dani the main thing was having him home again in the yellow house on their street, so her life could be happy again.

With spaghetti for dinner.

And stories in bed…

…and then: "Good night,
good night! And sleep well, Amore!"

That's what they say in Italy, where Dani's father
comes from.

On the first evening home for Dani's father Gianni, everything was exactly as Dani wanted it to be, except that he was in a bit of a hurry over her third goodnight hug.

Suddenly he wanted to watch Italian football on TV.

In Italy they are very good at football.

They have three top teams: Juventus, Napoli and Milan, and Milan was playing, the team her father liked best.

Of course he had to watch the game! Of course she understood.

After a little while Dani tiptoed out of bed to give him another hug.

When she came into the living room he had turned down the TV and was talking on the phone.

He stopped, surprised.

"You're not asleep yet?"

But just then Milan's forward scored a goal!

Dad was excited and Dani left him with the TV and his phone.

Chapter 2

Next morning he made her lunch and followed her out to the gate.

"Bye, Dani! Have fun at Skansen!" he called, waving.

Dani walked backwards, waving, till she bumped into a lamp post…

...and fell flat on the ground!

Her father came limping after her.

"Are you all right?"

"I'm fine." Dani smiled and picked herself up.

She was about to carry on her backwards walk when her father stopped her.

"Dani…" he said, "would you mind if Sadie popped in to see us after work?"

He meant the nurse he'd met at the hospital over the summer.

"What for?" she asked.

"She'd love to make us a delicious meal!"

"Doesn't have to," said Dani. "You're such a good cook yourself!"

That was true. Dani's father is phenomenal at cooking. Especially spaghetti.

"Please, Dani," he pleaded, "tell me Sadie's welcome."

Dani looked at him.

Then she turned around and kept walking.

Forwards.

Without looking back.

Chapter 3

When she got to school the whole class was gathered
in the playground. The teacher was telling everyone
the rules of the trip.

"No one is to run off on their own and get lost,"
she said. "But in the unlikely event that this should
happen…"

She broke off and looked at them sternly.

"What should you do?"

Cushion put up his hand. "Panic."

That wasn't right.

"You wait where you last saw the class until
someone comes and finds you."

Everyone nodded.

"Wait there, even if it takes a little while. Just be patient!"

Everyone nodded again.

"Then let's go!"

They formed a line and headed for the bus.

Walking in line is something Dani's class is good at. No other class does it so nicely.

Hand in hand they went, walking briskly.

Cushion's father was driving them. He has his own bus company.

Cushion was allowed to sit in the seat beside him and speak into the microphone.

"Welcome aboard!" he said once the bus had started.

"Now we're leaving Solna and heading towards Skansen," he continued, when the bus was out on the main road. "Skansen is Stockholm's largest zoo, where you can see woolly bears and wolves and old houses from the olden days."

Everyone was impressed by how good he sounded.

To start with, the trip went well. They all talked
and sang.

Then Jonathan started to feel sick.

Then everyone started to feel sick.

Cushion handed out bags in case anyone vomited.

Luckily they soon arrived and they could all get off.

Chapter 4

First they went and looked at the old buildings, which had been moved to Skansen from different parts of Sweden.

For example, there was a schoolhouse from the days when no one had money for paper and pens.

"Children had to write on a blackboard," said a guide, dressed as an olden days schoolteacher. "And they had to rub things out with a rabbit's foot."

She passed around some blackboards and cut-off rabbits' feet so they could really understand what things were like then.

"Imagine sitting with your backside on the seat where someone sat a hundred years ago!" said Vicky.

"Yeah, imagine you sitting there farting!" giggled Benny.

"We're not farting!" Mickey shrieked, and flew up from her seat to clonk him with her blackboard.

"We never fart!" Vicky hissed.

They were behaving so badly, the guide intervened.

"Let's focus on how it was in the old days," she urged them, raising her pointing stick.

"Back then, if children misbehaved, they were hit over the fingers with a ruler," the guide continued.

"Does anyone want to try that?" their teacher asked.

They all calmed down.

Then they all went to look at the animals.

They saw the wolverines, the wild boars, and the seals.

And then they ate their picnic lunches, before the highlight of the day: the Skansen aquarium!

There were not just fish. There were frogs and spiders and snakes.

Some snakes lay tangled up in one big ball.

A little way away stood a zookeeper with a boa constrictor.

"I'll bet there's no one here who dares to pat this cutie," she said.

The class answered with silence.

But suddenly there was a voice: "Yes, me!"

It was Dani.

The class looked admiringly at her.

"Good for you!" said the zookeeper.

Dani touched the boa constrictor carefully. It felt smooth and dry.

"Bravo!" said the zookeeper. "Does anyone else want to try?"

No one did.

"Then I appoint you the bravest in the class," said the zookeeper.

Everyone nodded, except Vicky and Mickey.

.

Then, when Dani went to look at the monkeys, they stood in front of her.

"Don't come here!" giggled Vicky. "Don't bother looking."

"Why not?" Dani asked.

"Because you might as well look in the mirror," giggled Mickey.

Why did they say that?

Did they think Dani looked like a monkey?

In that case it was not a nice thing to say!

Dani likes monkeys a lot, but that doesn't mean she wants to look like one.

It wasn't nice for the monkeys either!

Surely they don't want to look like people?

Everyone wants to look like themselves.

When Dani felt tears welling up, she turned
and rushed away.

Her eyes were blurred.

Chapter 5

She ran until she almost fell over a big fat goose
waddling along the path.

She slowed down and walked beside it.

Dani had been to Skansen many times before. Especially when she was living with her grandmother and grandfather.

That was when her mother had died and her father was so unhappy that he couldn't look after her.

Grandma and Grandpa had done it instead.

They tried lots of things to keep Dani from being unhappy too.

Every Sunday they took her to Skansen. That's how Dani knew all the animals.

But she hadn't met this goose before.

It was black and white with some red on its beak.

A group of tourists asked if they could take
a picture of the pretty pair.

When they'd finished they bowed and thanked
Dani and gave her a bag of sweets.

And the goose waddled on.

Suddenly Dani remembered: the class!

Where had they gone to? Was she separated from them now?

She did exactly what Cushion had said—she panicked.

But then she remembered the teacher's words:

"Wait where you last saw the class until someone comes and finds you!"

chapter 6

Dani ran all the way back to the aquarium…

But the class was no longer there.

She went out again and looked around.

Where had they all gone?

The sun was hot. It was autumn, but today it was as if summer had returned to say a really warm farewell.

Dani wiped her forehead and sat in the shade of a tree. She had a good view of the aquarium.

Now she mustn't panic but wait calmly until someone came to find her.

Just be patient, the teacher had said.

Soon someone in the class would wonder:

"Where's Dani?"

And the teacher would ask who had seen her last.

And Vicky would put her hand up and call out: "Me and Mickey!"

And Mickey would say: "It was when she wanted to look at the monkeys and we happened to say something stupid…"

And Vicky would say: "But we were only joking."

And the teacher would say: "Stop talking now. Run and look for her!"

Then Vicky and Mickey would find her and say sorry and everything would be fine, Dani thought, and she ate a sweet.

But no one came. It seemed no one had missed her.

Dani ate another sweet and desperately tried to think of something else.

Of Ella, her friend who had moved away.

And everything immediately felt a bit better. That's always the way when Dani thinks of Ella.

The sweets tasted very good. She took a third. And a fourth. And a fifth. And then she wiped her forehead again.

But nothing happened, except that some crows started squabbling over a bit of sausage someone had dropped.

After a while an angry woman came over and told Dani to pick up all the papers and scraps she'd scattered around her.

Dani did as the woman said.

"Gosh it's hard to be patient," she muttered as she picked up everyone else's mess.

Then her patience ran out. So did the sweets.

And at last something happened!

A school class came charging up the hill, but it wasn't hers. It was another one with children who shrieked and shouted.

I wouldn't want to be in that class, Dani thought, taking care not to get in the way of the wild crowd.

But right at the back she caught sight of someone who seemed familiar. A girl who didn't walk like the others, but hopped instead.

First two steps and then hop! Then two steps more and hop!

There was only one person Dani knew who moved like that.

It wasn't… No, it couldn't be true!

Or, maybe!

Yes…

YES!!!

"ELLA!" shrieked Dani.

The girl stopped. When she saw Dani she let out a shriek of delight.

And they flew towards each other!

"What are you doing here?"
cried Dani.

"I'm on a class trip."

"I'm here with
my class, too!"

Ella looked around her.

"What have you done with them?"

Dani was serious again.

"They lost me. Or rather, I lost them!"

"How lucky that you found me! What shall we play?"

Ella always asked that. As soon as they saw each other!

Dani didn't know what to answer. She was still too surprised.

Ella was hopping impatiently up and down.

"Come on, let's hide."

Dani hesitated.

"Can you? What if your teacher notices…"

"She never does!" Ella assured her. "As long as the others don't see me leaving the line."

That made Dani smile.

"Do you call that a line?"

Five boys had fallen into a heap on the ground,
where they lay wrestling, almost as tangled as the
aquarium snakes.

When the Northbrook teacher rushed over to pull
them up, Ella grabbed Dani.

"Now. No one will see us. Are you ready?"

Without waiting for an answer, she was off.

What should Dani do?

Follow her best friend in the whole
world or do as the teacher had said?

The first, of course!

Dani let go of her worries and followed.

Chapter 7

Every time Ella and Dani get together they find a fun new game to play.

This time they rushed to the old schoolhouse where they decided that Ella was a strict schoolteacher from the olden days and Dani was a pupil who hadn't done her homework.

"What's seventy-eight times eighty-nine?" asked the teacher from the olden days.

When Dani couldn't answer
she got a rap on the knuckles
with a pretend ruler.

Then she had to stand in the dunce's corner and pretend to cry. She was good at that.

She cried so hard that a security guard came in to see.

"Little friend," he said anxiously, "what's the matter?"

"It's not as bad as it sounds," said Ella. "She's just pretending."

"Are you sure?"

Ella nodded and put a protective arm around Dani.

The guard muttered something and turned to go, but stopped in the doorway.

"Have you by any chance seen a girl who's lost her class?" he asked.

"No," said Ella decidedly. "We have not!"

And the guard went away.

"We're best friends!" Ella called after him.

"Best friends in the whole world!" Dani corrected her.

That's how she feels. And she thinks the words sound better.

They stood and watched until he was gone.

Then Ella turned to Dani again.

"Did you notice that I said have not?" she asked.

"That's how they said it in the olden days."

Chapter 8

But that game was finished and after a little while they left the schoolhouse.

"That was me he was talking about," Dani sighed.

"You can't be sure," Ella said. "Every day hundreds of children get lost at Skansen. Didn't you know that?"

"Every day?"

"Yeah, or every second day."

"What happens to them?"

"They get thrown to the bears. Didn't they warn you about that in my old class?"

Dani thought about it.

"No. The teacher only said that if we got lost we should go and stand where they saw us last."

"Well, did you do that?"

"Yes."

"Well then. You did it right," said Ella.

"I have to go back now in any case," Dani sighed.

But Ella didn't think so.

"Let's just play a little bit more."

"What then?"

"A treasure hunt, I was thinking. What do you think about that?"

Dani didn't answer.

"Did you hear what I said?" asked Ella.

"Yes, you said a treasure hunt. But…"

"But what?"

"Is there any treasure here we can dig up?"

"Not yet. First we have to bury it. Come on!"

But Dani resisted.

"I don't understand. What shall we bury?"

"The best thing we have, of course," Ella explained.

"And what is that?"

"Something we have with us. Have a look!"

Dani put her hands in her pockets and came up with a fistful of sweet wrappers.

"No, not that," said Ella. "I mean this!"

She held out her necklace—the one with half of a silver heart.

Dani had the other half.

Dani shook her head.

Every morning she put on her necklace and she wore it the whole day until it was time for bed.

"I'll never in my life leave that here!" she said.

But Ella didn't give up:

"It's much safer if it's buried. One of us might lose half of the heart otherwise! What would happen then, do you think?"

"I don't know…"

"Broken friendship. Have you ever thought of that?"

No, Dani hadn't. In fact, never.

Ella stared at her.

"Do you really want to take that risk?"

Dani pressed her lips tight and they walked in silence until they reached the moose enclosure.

Dani stopped to look at the moose, which lay on the ground looking sad.

"It can't be much fun being a Skansen moose when you're really king of the forest," she said.

But Ella had already gone on.

Dani hurried after her.

"Where are we going actually?" she asked.

"To the bear mountain. If we bury the necklaces there the bears can guard them for us!"

Dani swallowed.

"Not really, though," she tried. "You mean pretend, don't you?"

But Ella was already on her way.

Dani followed reluctantly.

Soon they were at the bear mountain, but there were no bears to be seen. They had all gone into their caves to cool off.

"They're probably having a catnap," said Ella.

"Except it should be called a bearnap," said Dani.

"Maybe." Ella looked thoughtfully at the barrier around the bear mountain.

"This looks a bit hard to get over," she said in the end. "I think we'll go to the wolves instead."

She hurried on. Dani trotted after her.

But the wolves were also nowhere to be seen.

"Maybe they're also having a catnap," Ella said.

"Or a wolfnap," Dani corrected her. "You can't have a catnap if you're a wolf."

Ella wasn't listening. She had just caught sight of the guard again and pointed.

"Pretend not to see him!" she whispered.

They hurried away from the wolf area.

"Excuse me, girls!" called the guard.

They walked faster.

"Hello!" he called again. "Can I talk to you?"

Ella started walking even faster. Dani too. But when they turned around, they saw that he was right on their heels.

They sneaked off on small paths to lose him. But they lost themselves instead.

When they stopped to catch their breath, they found themselves on a little cobblestone street with old wooden houses and shops.

They have these also at Skansen, so you can see how the streets looked in the olden days.

"Why are we running, actually?" Dani asked. "The guard might be nice."

"We're running because that's part of it," puffed Ella.

Yes, of course, Dani thought. We almost always run in our games.

But this didn't feel like much of a game.

Ella crept into the garden of one of the houses.

"Come on, Dani!" she called. "This is the place we've been looking for!"

Chapter 9

Ella had found a lovely little garden.

In one corner was a bed of roses, still in full bloom.

"This will be good," she explained, picking up a piece of broken pot. "I can use this to dig with."

"What shall I do?" asked Dani.

"Keep watch. You have to warn me if the guard comes."

"But…"

"We're doing as I say!"

Dani went and stood at the corner of the house and Ella climbed in amongst the thorny rose bushes.

Soon you could hear her sighing and ouching.

"Ow ow!" she said. "What murdering thorns!
Ouch!"

But then she quietened, crouched down and
began to dig.

After a while she looked up happily:

"Come and see, Dani!"

Dani went over and inspected the hole.

"Nice work, eh?"

"Ye-es…"

"Now we take off our necklaces."

Ella undid her chain but Dani still hesitated.

"No," she mumbled. "I don't want to."

Ella looked sternly at her.

"You know what I said!"

"But I…"

"No buts!"

Dani took off her necklace unwillingly and passed it over. Their eyes met.

Then Ella put the two heart halves on the ground. She laid them close together so they made a whole heart.

Ella had got what she wanted. Soon she would say that the game was over.

But Ella didn't say anything as she solemnly filled in the hole.

"Say after me now, Dani," she asked. "Rest in peace, dear hearts!"

Dani cleared her throat.

"Rest in peace, dear hearts," she repeated.

"Now no one can keep us apart!" Ella chanted.

"Now no one can keep us apart…"

"Not even death!" continued Ella.

They got no further before they were interrupted by wild shouting in the street.

"Go and see what that is, Dani!"

Dani ran back and peeked around the corner of the house.

Ella's class was stampeding along the cobblestones.

They rushed into the various buildings and houses—then out again.

"What are they up to now?" wondered Ella, who had come out to have a look.

chapter 10

At that moment a girl with long hair caught sight of her.

"The-eeere! There she is," she yelled. "I've found her!"

Ella backed away, but the girl with the plaits
ran after her and grabbed her.

Soon Ella was surrounded by her classmates.
They took hold of her and dragged her
off as if she was a thief.

Dani stood there as if she'd
been turned to stone.

Only catching sight of
the guard helped her
move again and she ran
into the garden to hide
amongst the rose bushes.

The thorns ripped and tore at her, but she kept going, then sank down on her knees and stayed completely still.

He still managed to find her.

Soon she saw his big boots coming across the garden…

He pulled branches aside and stood there looking at her.

"Is your name Dani?" he asked.

Dani hummed something, which could sound like both yes and no.

Dani was the name her mother gave her when she was born, because she was so small and fine. But her name was really Daniela.

"What did you say?" asked the guard.

"My name is Daniela, but I'm called Dani."

"Good then!" said the guard, looking pleased.
"You're the one I'm looking for! Come on, let's go to
your teacher. Or would you rather stay with us here
at Skansen?"

No, Dani didn't want to stay. She wanted to go home to her father.

"I'm coming," she said. "I just have to dig something up. Could you move over a bit? You're in the way."

The guard moved and Dani began to dig in the earth.

Soon she felt a necklace between her fingers and pulled it up. Then she found the other necklace too.

She put them in her pocket.

"Have you finished?" asked the guard.
"We need to hurry."

He held out his big hand. Dani took it
and off they went—he with normal
steps and she with short but fast ones.
Soon they reached the escalator
leading to Skansen's front gates.

Chapter 11

No one saw the lonely creature creeping over to the rose bushes where the treasure was buried.

It was Ella. Somehow she had managed to escape from her captors.

Now she dropped to all fours, crept into the prickly tangle and felt with her hands.

She groped around thoroughly, till she gave up and crept out again.

"Dani," she called. "Where are you?"

Her voice sounded desolate in the stillness of the garden. She sniffed.

"Dani, come out! Our friendship's in danger!"

But no Dani appeared.

She was on her way to the gates where her teacher was waiting.

Chapter 12

Even from a distance you could see that the teacher was angry.

"Where have you been?" she said grimly.

Dani was frightened. Never before had her teacher been angry with her.

"I got lost…" she started.

"No, we will discuss that later," the teacher interrupted. "The class is sitting in the bus, waiting."

She turned to the guard:

"Excuse me if I sound angry, but this is a teacher's nightmare. You count the children—and suddenly there's one missing! You ask the others, but no one knows anything…"

"Not even Vicky and Mickey?" Dani squeaked.

The teacher paused.

"No," she said. "Are they mixed up in this?"

Dani didn't answer.

And the teacher turned again to the guard.

"Thank you so much for your help!"

"No problem," said the guard. "You'd better hurry now!"

The teacher took Dani's hand and they ran the whole way to the bus.

"Here I come with the lost lamb," she puffed as they drew up.

The whole class clapped and cheered and Cushion's father said: "What a relief! Can we go now?"

"Yes, let's go," said the teacher and she sank into a seat. "Sit here, Dani!"

She patted the empty place beside her.

"Now I want you to tell me what happened. Did Mickey and Vicky have something to do with this?"

Dani shrugged.

"Answer me!" said the teacher. "What happened? Tell the truth now!"

"They were dumb," Dani admitted. "But it doesn't matter. Otherwise I wouldn't have met Ella."

"Ella? No, now listen…" the teacher protested.

At that moment there was banging on the door.

Cushion's father was just about to swing out but he hesitated, looking at the teacher.

"Are there any more lost lambs?"

"No, we have them all now," said the teacher, "but you'd better open the door."

The door opened and Ella hopped in, her face red from crying.

A murmur ran through the class.

"I just wanted to say something to Dani," she began with a croaky voice, looking around.

But seeing all the faces of her old class she forgot some of what she meant to say.

"Hello, Cushion! Hello, Meatball!"

She raised her hand and waved a little. Then she turned to her old teacher. "Can I come with you?"

"But young woman!" cried the teacher. "We're not even going in the same direction…"

She got no further before someone else stepped up onto the bus.

It was Ella's teacher.

"Ella!" she shouted. "What are you doing here?"

And Ella remembered the reason.

"I just had to tell Dani something."

"And you thought it was fine to disappear again?"

Ella drew herself up. "I'm not disappeared. I'm right here, as you can very well see!"

The teacher's mouth tightened.

"This is the second time she's left the class in one day," she complained. "This girl is crazy!"

"No, not crazy. Just a little headstrong and full of ideas," said her old teacher.

The Northbrook teacher sniffed, took hold of the truant and forced her toward the door.

Ella resisted and held tight to Dani, who was running after them.

"Dani!" she cried. "Our friendship's in danger!"

But the teacher from Northbrook took her away.

"When will we see each other again?" yelled Ella.

"We'll see…" began Dani, but she didn't know what else to say.

"You'll see you when you see you," Cushion tried, to help out.

The Northbrook teacher lifted Ella out through the door the way you lift an old Christmas tree on its way to the dump.

Dani's teacher looked out through the bus window.

"That's not looking good," she muttered.

Dani watched, too, though she would rather have closed her eyes. Everyone stared out the window.

But soon Ella was out of sight.

The journey home continued in silence.

The teacher didn't seem to be angry any more.

"And I thought you were making things up!" was all she said. "There's still a lot for an old fox to learn."

"Fox?" Dani looked at her.

"So they say," answered the teacher.

Dani nodded.

It wasn't always clear what people meant. But one thing was clear: Ella wasn't happy. Ella was sad.

And so Dani was too.

PART 2

Chapter 13

That's how it was for Dani at the start of her second
year at school following the class trip to Skansen.

Once they'd come back on the bus and been
let out at school, she trudged home.

She was tired, and all she wanted was to
see her father.

At least they'd be
together again.

But that's not what happened.

As she was entering the yellow house, she could hear happy voices coming from the living room. Her father was sitting on the sofa with Sadie.

"Ciao, Daniela!" he called.

That means hello in Italian.

He was clearly in his Italian mood.

"Hi Dani." Sadie smiled.

Dani tried to hide her disappointment.

"Could I have a hug?" asked her father.

Dani saw that the table was set as if they were
having a party, with tall glasses and bright napkins.
A wonderful smell wafted from the kitchen.

"Are you hungry?" Sadie asked hopefully.

Without waiting for an answer she got up and
went out to the kitchen to fetch the dinner.

Dani watched her go.

"What are we having?" she asked suspiciously.

"You'll see." Her father was beaming.

And there stood Sadie in the
doorway with a big roast
chicken on a plate.

Dani's face turned thunderous.

"What's the matter now?" asked her father.

"I don't eat babies," said Dani.

"Babies?"

"Chickens are hen's babies! Don't you know that?"

"Since when do you not eat chicken?"

"Since summer."

It was true. In the summer holidays Dani and Ella had sworn a holy oath never to eat meat from animals that hadn't had a chance to grow up and be big.

That was fine on the island with Ella's mother and stepfather Paddy, but it clearly wasn't the case back home.

"With us, you eat the food that's served," declared her father.

"But Ella and I…" Dani tried.

Her father flared up. "Basta!"

Italian again! That means:

That's enough!

Dani felt her bottom

lip begin to tremble.

She had stopped crying a long time ago, but of course now and then tears still rose inside her. It could happen once or twice a day. She swallowed to keep them down.

She was about to sit down when her father noticed her dirty hands. Dani had to go and wash them.

She scrubbed her fingers long and hard, but when she came back her father still didn't seem satisfied.

"Did you ever thank Sadie for the trip you went on?" he asked.

Some weeks earlier, when her father was still in hospital, Sadie had taken Dani and Ella to visit her sister who had Iceland ponies.

"Thanks after it happened," muttered Dani.

"You haven't told me a thing about it," her father continued. "Did you have fun?"

"Not much," answered Dani.

Her father wrinkled his forehead.

"Why not?"

Dani didn't answer.

The excursion to the Iceland ponies had been a catastrophe, but he didn't know that.

Chapter 14

This is how it had gone.

Lisette, Sadie's sister, wasn't at home when they arrived, but it didn't matter.

Sadie was used to looking after the ponies and there were two ponies in the stable that Lisette had brought in from the field.

"This is Vilda." Sadie pointed to a brown mare.

Then she pointed to a little, fat pony with a long mane. "And that's Shaggy."

Ella went straight up and patted the ponies but Dani stayed at a respectful distance.

"Which one would you like to ride on?" Sadie asked her.

"I don't know," said Dani. "Maybe that one."

She pointed to the fat pony.

"Shaggy." said Sadie. "Would you like Shaggy?"

"Yes, because isn't Vilda wild?" said Dani.

"Both are quiet and calm…" said Sadie.

"I'll take the fat one anyway," Dani decided. "He probably can't run very fast."

"Don't be so sure of that!" Sadie laughed. "Shaggy can be quick when he wants to."

What did she mean? You could hear in the name that Vilda was the wild one.

Sadie saddled up the ponies and led them out of the stable yard. There she helped Dani mount and made sure that everything was as it should be before she went to Ella.

Dani looked nervously around. The day was grey and windy. Big dark clouds loomed over the trees.

Ella didn't need any help. She goes to riding school and is almost as used to ponies as she is to guinea pigs.

She sprang up into the saddle, shortened her stirrups, gathered up the reins and waited impatiently to head for the riding track.

"Bravo, Ella," said Sadie. "We'll follow you with Shaggy."

She took hold of the reins.

"I'll lead him to start with. Sit up straight, Dani!"

Dani sat up straight.

As long as Sadie led Shaggy around the big riding track, everything went well.

But when they had been walking for a bit, Sadie said: "I'll let you go now and stand in the middle. Is that all right?"

"Yes," said Dani. "Yes, I think so."

But Sadie had hardly stepped away before Shaggy stopped to eat a tuft of grass. He was obviously hungry.

"Come on," called Sadie. "Use your heels, Dani!"

Dani knew what using your heels meant because Ella had taught her. You dig your heels into the pony's sides. Then the pony knows it's time to go.

Dani kicked gently, but Shaggy didn't budge.

"Give him a good kick," Sadie yelled.

Dani kicked harder.

Nothing happened except that Shaggy snatched at another tuft of grass.

Sadie came running back.

"Has he had anything to eat today?" Dani wondered.

"Yes, he has," said Sadie. "Off you go now, Shaggy!"

Shaggy lifted his head and glared at her, but he began to plod.

And they went around the riding track again.

Round and round.

Far up ahead, Vilda was walking with sprightly steps.

Now and then Ella turned around and waved happily to Dani.

Still, Dani felt worry growing inside her.

Suddenly Shaggy stopped again.

This time Sadie didn't notice. She was standing in the middle again, facing Ella who was tired of walking and had begun to trot instead.

Dani thought it was nice to sit still for a change. She looked around in the wind.

That's when it happened.

Something rustled up behind them and a black plastic bag swept by.

Shaggy threw up his head and his ears went back.

Then everything happened lightning fast! Shaggy wheeled around and took off at a gallop.

Ponies can get very frightened if something unexpected turns up, even if it's only an empty bag.

Terrified, Dani clung to the saddle.

"Pull on the reins, Dani!" Ella yelled.

But Dani had already lost the reins. And the stirrups, for that matter.

She managed to clutch onto Shaggy's mane, until he stopped short and bucked.

Then she flew off…

… and landed with a hard thump on the ground.

She lay there absolutely still, with her eyes closed.

Sadie was beside her at once.

"Dani," Sadie cried, sinking to her knees. "Can you hear me?"

Dani didn't answer.

Ella reined in her pony, dropped to the ground and rushed over.

"What if Dani's broken her neck?" she panted.

"No, she hasn't," said Sadie. "But I think she's fainted."

"Help!" said Ella. "Wake up, Dani!"

Dani opened one eye and tried to sit up, but Sadie stopped her.

"Keep still!"

"You did a somersault in the air," Ella explained.

Dani looked at Ella and smiled weakly.

"Did I?"

"Yes, you sure did!" said Ella.

"Do you feel sick?" Sadie asked.

"A little," admitted Dani, looking at Shaggy, who was wandering around eating grass as if nothing had happened.

She tried to get up again, but Sadie held her back.

"You must lie absolutely still. You might have a concussion," said Sadie, making a sort of cushion for Dani out of her jacket.

Dani sank back with her head on it.

For the rest of the time she just lay and watched Ella, who got Vilda to trot around the track, round and round.

Ella rode so beautifully on Vilda that it was a pleasure to watch her.

Dani relaxed and enjoyed it.

But they hadn't told Dani's father any of this.

Even Dani hadn't said a single word.

Nor had Sadie. She hardly dared to think what could have happened to Dani.

How could she explain it to Gianni?

Only now, when he was home and sitting with them at the dinner table, did she decide to say exactly what had happened.

But there was no chance because suddenly the doorbell rang.

Who could it be?

"Dani, go and open the door," said her father.

Chapter 15

On the doorstep stood Grandma and Grandpa and Dani's cousin Sven.

"We just wanted to pop in and see how your father is," her grandfather explained.

"He's in there." Dani nodded towards the living room where her father was talking in a low voice to Sadie.

"Is someone else here?" asked Grandma.

"Yes…"

Grandma and Grandpa stepped into the hall and peeked into the living room.

Grandma's face fell.

But Grandpa
brightened up.
And Sven asked
what smelled so good.
   "It's Sadie's roast
chicken," said Dad.
"Come and try some!"

Grandpa collected
more chairs and
Sadie quickly set
three more places.

Then Dad carved the chicken and everyone had to hold out their plates.

But just as he went to put a chicken wing on Dani's, she pulled it away…

…and the wing landed on the tablecloth.

Dani's father went red in the face.

"That is not okay, Dani!" he thundered.

And Dani burst into tears.

"It's not so bad!" said Sadie, taking away the wing. "I'll go and heat up a corncob for Dani."

As soon as Sadie had disappeared into the kitchen, Grandma started:

"Why is she here, Gianni?" she asked. "Don't you understand that Dani wants her father to herself for once?"

"Not necessarily," said Dad. "And anyway, we talked about it this morning. Didn't we, Dani? You're pleased that Sadie's here, aren't you?"

Dani stared at the tablecloth where a stain was spreading.

"It doesn't seem so." Grandpa sounded worried.

"How could I be happy…" she sniffed.

"Yes, how could she be?" Grandma agreed.

"…when Ella's unhappy?"

"Ella?" said Grandpa in surprise.

"What has she got to do with this?" Dani's father was just as surprised.

But they weren't going to find out.

Dani left the table and rushed to her room and slammed the door.

Chapter 16

Snow and Flake the guinea pigs jumped when the door slammed and started chittering. Now something was really wrong!

"Don't be frightened." Dani tried to calm them and she took them out of their cage.

She dug in her pockets for something nice for them to eat, but there were none of the usual sunflower seeds, only a handful of sweet wrappers.

And the necklaces!

"Maybe you want to hear what happened at Skansen today?" she said. "You're probably the only ones interested in my life!"

The guinea pigs pricked their ears.

But they weren't going to hear the story either. Dani fell silent, listening to the talk in the living room.

It sounded as if Grandma and Grandpa had teamed up.

She tiptoed to the door and opened it a little bit.

"Ella this and Ella that! I never hear anything but Ella!" her father yelled.

"That's not so strange," Grandma said coldly, "who else has she got? Only her grandfather and me! And a father who behaves like a complete idiot!"

"Gianni doesn't mean any harm!" Grandpa tried to calm her. "He's just in love and a bit distracted."

"She's got me too," said Sven.

"And her friends at school!" Grandpa suggested.

"What friends? You don't mean those two ratbags who are constantly trying to pinch her?"

Dani closed the door again, but it wasn't long before Sven opened it.

"Can I come in? I just want to know why Ella's unhappy."

"Because she has such horrible classmates!" said Dani. "And a teacher who says she's crazy…"

"You don't think she is?" Sven wondered.

"Of course she's not! But she might be, if no one does anything."

Sven didn't understand, and he wasn't all that interested either. He just wanted Dani to come out to the others in the living room.

"Let's call Ella's extra father," he suggested, and pulled his phone from his pocket.

"Paddy will sort it out. I have his number."

Dani's mouth fell open.

"Do you usually call him?"

"Can happen," said Sven.

"How often?"

"Two or three times a day. We're friends."

"Are you?"

After the visit to the island in the summer Sven counted Paddy as his extra father too, but Dani didn't know that.

It had begun when he was allowed to drive Paddy's motorboat and continued when they had put the nets out together. And then Paddy gave Sven his telephone number.

He tapped in the number and turned on the speaker.

"Hi Sven!" came Paddy's voice. "It's been a while! You haven't called for several hours!"

"I know, I haven't had time."

"Has something happened?"

"Yeah, it seems so. Dani met Ella at Skansen, and she says she's going crazy."

"I know…" Paddy sighed. "She's in a bad class."

"Can't you do something about it?" Sven asked.

"I've tried," said Paddy.

"Have you talked to her teacher?"

"Absolutely. Ella's mother and I have both talked to her. Many times. But it doesn't help."

"Then she needs to change class. Or school," said Sven. "I did that. Then it was better."

"Is that right? That's probably the best idea."

Dani nodded in agreement.

But all that would take time. Was there nothing they could do for Ella right now?

Suddenly she had an idea. She left Sven to finish his conversation with Paddy and she hurried back to the living room.

Chapter 17

The atmosphere at the table was tense and Sadie
was nowhere to be seen.

Where was she?

Dad reached out to Dani.

"Sit here with me!" he pleaded. "It's so long since
I had my little girl on my knee!"

Dani wriggled, but he held on.

"Grandma says it's my fault that you're unhappy."

"Let go!" said Dani and she managed to free herself.

She went to the kitchen where she found Sadie
washing the dishes.

Dani got straight to the point.

"Will you do something for me, Sadie?"

"What is it?" asked Sadie, lifting a plate to be rinsed.

"Can you take me and Ella to the Iceland ponies again?"

Sadie almost dropped the plate, but she caught and held it under running water.

"Do you really want to go riding again?" she asked.

"No, not me," Dani explained, "but Ella. I'll just watch."

Sadie turned off the tap and put the plate to one side.

"Aha," she said. "I see. You want to make Ella happy?"

"That's right…"

"Because then you'll be happy too?"

"Yes. Very happy."

Sadie thought for a moment.

"I am actually going to my sister's on Saturday."

She thought again.

"So why shouldn't you come too?" she said finally. "Let's do that…"

Dani lit up. And she remembered to say thank you.

"Thank you!" she said. "Thanks in advance, Sadie! You don't know how much this means to me."

Then she helped Sadie dry all the glasses that were left and put them away in the cupboard, before sitting at the kitchen table to eat the corncob Sadie had heated up for her.

Chapter 18

And then it was dessert: ice cream with meringue and hot chocolate sauce.

"I still haven't heard a thing about the Iceland pony expedition," Dad reminded them.

"We're going back again soon," Sadie told him.

"Is that right? So it was a great success!"

"Let's concentrate on the ice cream," said Dani. So they did.

Then Sven told his latest riddles. The first went like this:

"What can everyone see but no one touch?"

"Smoke," guessed Sadie.

"Correct!" said Sven. "Now for the next: Who never misses a ball?"

"Dani," guessed Dani's grandpa.

"Wrong!" said Sven.

"The wall," Sadie guessed.

"Correct!" The third riddle: Who's been around the world the most times?"

But they were interrupted again by Dani's father. He wanted to know if they thought the chicken had tasted good.

"Not bad," Grandma admitted, and she started leafing through one of his Italian newspapers lying on the sofa.

She was trying to learn Italian so she could travel with Dani to Rome to meet Dani's grandmother and cousins.

"The chicken was excellent!" said Grandpa, turning on the TV to see the news.

"The corn was also excellent!" said Dani. "The tastiest corn I've ever eaten!"

"Who's been around the world the most times?" Sven repeated impatiently.

"The moon," Sadie guessed.

"Correct again!" yelled Sven. "Sadie got them all right!"

"Fantastic, Sadie!" exclaimed Dani's father.

He didn't know that Sadie had read the riddles and answers on the same milk carton as Sven.

He thought Sadie really was smart!

Chapter 19

Moments later all the guests went home, including Sadie. And Dani was finally alone with her father.

"It all worked out well in the end," he said. "Don't you think, Dani?"

"What did?" Dani was watching the candle burning down.

"With Sadie."

"Oh," said Dani. "I thought you meant with the corncob."

"Don't you agree?" he persisted.

"Not bad," Dani admitted, sounding like her grandmother.

Her father sank into silence.

For a long time there was only the sound of the radio talking to itself out in the kitchen.

But suddenly Dani said: "What about Mama?"

Her father gave a start.

"Have you forgotten her now?"

"How could I forget her?"

"But you like Sadie?"

"Yes, I do. Very much."

He got up and Dani saw that he had tears in his eyes.

It still happened sometimes when Dani's mother was mentioned, even though it was nearly five years since she died.

He limped from the room and Dani went and lay on the sofa where Cat was waiting for her.

"How could I ever forget Ella?" she said, stroking its back.

The cat watched her thoughtfully.

"But I like you too," she hurried to add. "Very much."

She stretched out on the sofa and began to think up a little poem for Ella.

She does that sometimes, pulling small poems right out of the air.

Ella! Ella! You are my dearest!
Don't be unhappy, or I can't be happy.
If you're sad I'll break into a thousand pieces!

She stopped.

The poem didn't have a single rhyme but she was
pleased with it anyway, because it was true.

She was about to go on when the phone rang.

It was Ella, who had come back home and wanted
to speak to her. But it was almost impossible to hear
her because she was crying so hard.

"I j-just wanted to tell you s-something on the
bus," she sobbed. "S-someone has dug up our tr-tr-
treasure!"

Dani sank into the chair beside the telephone
table and laughed.

"I know!"

The sobbing stopped at once.

"How can you know that?"

"Because I'm the one who did it!"

It was a few seconds before Ella understood.

She gasped—and suddenly it was as if the sun
had come out after rain.

"Well done," she said and sniffed so loudly that it
hissed into the phone. "When did you say we'd see
each other again?"

This time Dani had the best possible answer:

"On Saturday. We can go with Sadie again to see the Iceland ponies."

Ella almost whinnied with happiness.

"I can manage till then."

"Do you mean with your class?"

"I mean with anything. As long as I can see you! Thank you, Dani! You've saved my life!"

"It was nothing," said Dani.

"Night night!"

"Night," said Dani, smiling happily.

Chapter 20

She was still smiling as she undressed and brushed her teeth and put on her nightie and lay in her comfy bed.

"It doesn't really matter so much that Sadie was here today," she explained when her father popped in. "I forgive you. This once."

"Thank you, Dani," said her father, putting the night cover over the guinea pigs.

"How was Skansen?" he suddenly remembered.

"Good," said Dani. "I met Ella."

Her father straightened up.

"Ella this and Ella that! How many children are there actually in your class?"

"Twenty-two," said Dani. "Why?"

"Then can't you find one of them to be friends with?"

"Mmm, I probably can," yawned Dani. "But not best friends in the world."

"But Dani, don't you understand? Children can't see each other very often when they live as far apart as you and Ella."

His cell phone rang.

"Just a minute," he said and took it out to the living room.

Dani reached out her arm and lifted the edge of the guinea pigs' cover.

"Did you hear that?" she whispered. "They always want to keep me and Ella apart! Always, always, always. But they can't, because we keep seeing each other!"

The guinea pigs chattered knowingly.

"If only you knew how happy you are when you're happy," continued Dani.

The guinea pigs looked at each other. What was she talking about now?

Guinea pigs always know how happy they are when they're happy. You can tell by the way their eyes glitter.

"Night night to you too!" Dani dropped the cover back and waited for her father.

Why was he taking so long on the phone?

"That was Sadie," he said when he finally came back. "She thinks I behaved badly with you today."

Dani closed her eyes.

Must he talk about that again? She had already forgiven him.

But her father went on. He was very upset.

"I didn't mean to. I never want to make you unhappy, Dani! Do you understand that?"

He looked beseechingly at her, but Dani wasn't listening. It had been a long day and she only wanted to sleep.

When he saw that, he tucked her in.

"Amore," he said, almost to himself. "I don't know what gets into me."

"Relax!" said Dani, and she rolled herself into a ball, just like Cat.

Her father turned out the light and crept from the room.

"Good night, Ella," Dani mumbled in the direction of Ella's house. "At last I can sleep. See you when I see you. No, I mean on Saturday!"

She thought a bit.

"I can manage till then, too," she added. "With anything."

And she fell asleep.

Have you read the other books about Dani?

Dani is probably the happiest person she knows. She's happy because she's going to start school. She's been waiting to go to school her whole life. Then things get even better—she meets Ella.

This is a story about Dani, who's always happy. She's unhappy too, now and then, but she doesn't count those times. But she does miss her best friend Ella, who moved to another town.

It's the second-to-last day of school and Dani's so happy she could write a book about it! In fact, that's exactly what she's done. But then she gets some bad news. How will she ever be happy again?

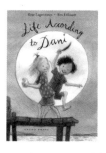

It's Dani's first summer break —her best one ever! Dani is staying on an island with Ella, her best friend in the world. They play all day long. They build huts, fish and spy on wild animals. They go swimming five, six, seven times a day.